Copyright

This is a work of fiction. Names, characters, places, and incidents are either products of the author's imagination or, if real, are used fictitiously.

Ebook Edition Copyright © 2013 by Robert Gannon
First Print Edition Copyring 2020 by Robert Gannon

All rights reserved.
No part of this book may be reproduced or transmitted in any form or by any means, electronic or mechanical, without written permission from the author, except for the use of brief quotations in a review.

Sketching Details
http://sketchingdetails.com

First Print Edition: 20 December 2020

Table of Contents

Once Upon a Time
Black Dirt Country
Take Out
Physics
Stone Cold
About the Author & Thank You

Once Upon a Time

Jamie-Boy loved horror stories. Words like "Prometheus" and "perambulating" made him smile, even if he didn't exactly understand what they meant. Just knowing they were in a scary book kept him reading.

Unfortunately, Jamie-Boy's parents didn't share his love for horror stories. They were afraid he would have nightmares. No matter how many times he expressed his bravery, Jamie-Boy would always have to return his latest discovery.

Even the local librarians weren't sure what to do with Jamie-Boy. They loved to help young readers. Some even considered it their life's work. But Jamie-Boy pushed the limits of their generosity and enthusiasm. They wanted to encourage readers; just not that kind of reader.

As soon as he was old enough to ride his bike alone, Jamie-Boy would tell his parents he was going to play with his friends. He always rode past the pick-up game of baseball and said "hi," though he never stayed. His friends just weren't interested in the horror stories. What could possibly be fun about books? If his friends had to be forced to do their reading for school, why would they willingly join Jamie-Boy at the library?

The librarians always wanted to ask him the same things. Why did he want to read those books so badly? Couldn't he stay in the children's section so he wouldn't need help getting the books down? Jamie-Boy stood vigilant in his requests given amongst the tall stacks of the fiction section, even if he barely stood tall enough to reach the third shelf.

He devoured a glut of horror fiction capable of leaving a connoisseur queasy. An overstuffed leather armchair provided passage on a trip around the world. He witnessed murder most foul in Paris, conspired on meticulously plotted revenge in London, even gazed at grotesque ghosts sowing souls in Salem. There was no stopping him. Jamie-Boy devoured the inked pages of the masters as if his life depended upon the wisdom hidden between the lines.

One cool morning, Jamie-Boy kissed his mother on the cheek and pedaled away on his bicycle. Riding past the field was a mere formality as his friends would be pressing their noses against windows while he read all day long.

Jamie-Boy dripped fresh rain all over the faded carpet of the library lobby. He was glad. Plenty of horror stories took place during storms so he guessed it could only enhance the experience. He wandered down the aisles, gazing at all the authors he read before: Beckford, and Brown, and Bronte, and the other Bronte. None of these were his favorites.

Jamie-Boy wondered if the reference desk librarian moved the Dickens holiday ghost anthology to eye height. She made him read A Christmas Carol in exchange for a James collection one time and he never forgave her. It had ghosts just like she promised but could hardly be considered a horror story.

Jamie-Boy was trying to find Shelley because he watched Frankenstein the night before and wanted to read more of her stories. Another book grabbed his eye. He didn't recognize the name as an author: Cthulhu. Jamie-Boy read across the shelf to Derleth before it hit him. The name was from Lovecraft, some kind of old monster from the sea. The long sentences and New England settings confused Jamie-Boy so he didn't really like those stories. He liked Lovecraft more than he liked Derleth, though. The strange ideas originated in Lovecraft's imagination, so they had to be the best. Jamie-Boy knew the older stories were always better because those writers came up with the ideas fist.

The book charged Jamie-Boy's attention. It stood out like his own presence in the library. The spine was covered in a dull red leather turned brown in spots. Tiny holes disturbed the spine, disguising the title behind the tireless work of small creatures gathering a well-tanned meal. Shelley would have to wait for another day.

Jamie-Boy stretched his body as far as he could to reach the book but only managed to tilt it on its side. The red leather was only on the spine. The rest was covered in a mixed blue and green linen. Gray thread rose above the cover in a marbled pattern of smoke and fog. Jamie-Boy struggled to pull the book from the shelf; the surprising weight wouldn't stop him from reading.

He traced his finger around the book, admiring the silver edge of the pages. A drop of water from his sleeve danced along the reflection in the fluorescent lighting as wandered over to his favorite leather chair. Jamie-Boy always read his stories there. It was close enough to the front desk to ask for help if he needed it but not so close as to draw any unnecessary attention to himself. He liked to be alone when he read.

Jamie-Boy cut his finger on the cover. The blood disappeared in the silver lining as he dropped the book on the floor. He licked his cut finger and looked for a librarian. No one was at the front desk. Jamie-Boy pressed his finger against the cold window and stared out at the parked cars. The lot was full but Jamie-Boy didn't hear anyone, only the crash of thunder outside.

His finger stopped bleeding. The book was still in front of the chair where he dropped it, even though he was sure someone else had walked by.

The cover was stuck with the strength of a high grade adhesive. Digging with all of his might, Jamie-Boy managed to slide his cut finger behind the cover.

Lightning flashed all around him. Jamie-Boy knew from his stories if he counted one two three four five six until the thunder sounded he would know how far away the storm was. The thunder didn't sound right. It was too soft. It felt wet, like an echo in the basement. Jamie-Boy still heard the noise when the thunder barked outside.

The silver edge seemed to change as the storm raged on. It became darker, glossier, less consistent from corner to corner. The pages rustled as Jamie-Boy pried with his finger against the stuck cover. Too heavy to hold any longer, the book flopped against his lap. Only then did Jamie-Boy realize he couldn't remove his finger from the book.

He took a deep breath and tried to relax. He was brave and smart. Horror stories couldn't hurt him. The writers were dead. The characters weren't real. This wasn't a nightmare. Jamie-Boy could control the situation. The storm just had him worked up and sent his mind racing. If he closed his eyes, there wouldn't be a problem. It was all in his imagination.

His arm went limp when he heard the crash. The first thing he noticed was his hand. The blue veins bounced faster than the rainfall beneath his pale skin. Every ounce of his skin shook and no conscious effort could stall the motion.

The fascination didn't last when Jamie-Boy saw the book was open on the floor. The ink dripped through the page in a vortex of words, racing down with the crimson drops from his hands. Pages collapsed into the growing darkness of loose phrases flowing over the edge.

Jamie-Boy met the monster's gaze as the puddle grew around his feet. It licked the dried blood from its largest mouth. Jamie-Boy threw his arm down to close the cover but the tentacle moved to quickly, wrapping his wrist tightly as the creature gained footing in the library. Its scales glistened a random pattern of silver and blue as the ink and formatting rushed to an actual physical presence. Jamie-Boy screamed with all his might, though the sound only registered as a weak whimper.

The creature rose taller than the fiction stacks, slinking the brave child past his idols with a firm grip around his waist. Jamie-Boy drifted through the currents of Cthulhu and landed on the top shelf. A book crashed upon it, opening to a Derleth story he always pushed aside. The monster locked his eye on Jamie-Boy and flashed rows of glistening fangs.

"Read me a good story, Jamie-Boy. This one's my favorite."

Black Dirt Country

My family used to go apple picking every October. We would wake up with the sun and drive for two hours into the black dirt region. Every home was a farm. They lived off the land. The tradition ended when we were all too busy. Our produce came pre-bagged from the supermarket and we never looked back.

There was one farm I always wanted to visit. The owners put on a big production every year. There were hay rides and apple pie. It was the only important stop.

For my twenty-second birthday, I only had one request. "I want to go to Black Dirt Country."

"Tom, you know they prefer the Black Dirt Region." My mother was crazy about semantics. "And why would you want to go back? You've seen Aunt Rose's letters."

"I also know what she told me last week. I asked if the Tasker Orchard was still open and she said it was better than ever."

"Again with the Tasker Orchard?" My father was frustrated. "Son, it's not that great. Their prices—"

"Does it always have to be about the price? We used to have fun there. You're the one who says we need to spend more time together."

That broke them. They agreed to the trip. We would go on the first Sunday in October. Everything would be perfect.

###

The winding interstate was built right through the mountains. It seemed like my memories sprung back to life. The trees hung golden over the roadway, framing the manicured mansions and small farmhouses along the way.

My seat belt kept my head from hitting the roof when I saw the sign:

Do Not Remove Earth.
The Black Dirt Is Our Livelihood.
Thieves Will Be Prosecuted.

We were here.

My father slowed the car. "Was the sign always that faded?"

Of course the sign was faded. The people had more important things to worry about.

"There doesn't seem to be much left." My mother was worried.

Doubt crept into my mind. Where were the roadside farm stands? We'd normally have gigantic five dollar pumpkins by now. There was nothing.

"How far is Aunt Rose's house?" I asked.

"Oh, she lives about an hour north of here. Good thing, too." My mother sighed. "The electric company still offers service up there."

So Aunt Rose wasn't exaggerating. They really did cut off the power. I looked out the rear window. It was like a fire waiting to happen. The crops were yellow, dried and bleached by the sun.

My father slammed on the breaks. "What the heck was that?"

I spun around. "It looks like…a cow?"

"It's a skeleton," he said. "We're turning around."

It was like he was trying to ruin my birthday. Why didn't they just say no to the whole thing before leaving?

"Wait." I grinned. "We're here."

The billboard for the Tasker Orchard was like a lost relic. It was immaculate. The portrait of the family was a funhouse mirror of us: mother, father, and son, happily picking apples.

A child with a flag knocked on the window. "Welcome. Do you have any goods in your car, sir?" He peered inside. "I see not. Follow the flags to the parking area. You're the first ones today." He fiddled with a walkie-talkie.

We stopped at the gravel lot. I couldn't see the farmhouse at all.

"Greetings, folks!" A man approached us. "Can I interest you in some apples today?"

Where were the trucks filled with hay? The fresh apple pie?

"If you follow me, I'll take you to our special selection." The man didn't wait for us to respond. "We began experimenting with our own unique breed of apples about ten years ago. We think we got it just right now."

The man leaned against a tree. This had to be the largest I'd ever seen. The fruit was pale pink, bigger than grapefruits.

"We call them Black Dirt Hybrids. All thanks to our special fertilizer on this gorgeous earth."

There was a stained burlap bag behind the tree. It smelled like salt.

Ow! Something hit my head. There was blood everywhere. I started to panic. I grabbed my head. It felt cold. It was ok. I wasn't hurt.

There was an apple split open on the ground. The flesh was red like meat and stunk like it was spoiled. My mother covered her nose.

"Why'd you waste that apple? We don't appreciate vandalism and thievery." The man pulled out a walkie-talkie. "Junior, we have a situation. Bring out the family." He approached my father. "I believe we have a bill to settle."

Take Out

I may not know a whole lot about cooking, but I do know this: food is not supposed to prepare itself. I'm not talking about those creepy self-heating soup cans, either. There's a pretty clear line between "press to heat" and knives flying through the air on their own.

My natural reaction was to run away. Fight is totally overrated. The only correct choice is flight when it prevents my face from becoming a fresh chopped salad. While the knives desire to provide extra protein for my diet was admirable, I'd much rather procure a different species for my nutritional needs. Perhaps a nice lean cut of beef or a juicy chicken breast straight off a restaurant grill.

Naturally, the natural reaction went out the door like a garbage bag full of empty take-away containers. The flashy knife flight reminded me of those food competitions on TV. There was never a real opportunity to taste the results no matter how good they looked. The only reasonable course of action was to call for a large pepperoni pizza, light on the sauce.

The fifteen minute delivery window gave me plenty of time to think. The crashing pots and bursts of flame seemed to cry out in protest. Why wait for delivery when I could be my own main course in seconds?

Maybe I was being paranoid. Flying knives and kitchen fireworks could mean many things. Like that drink after work was stronger than I thought. Or my dearly departed grandmother took pity upon my bachelorhood and decided to play Home-Ec teacher from beyond the grave. It did provide a better excuse for the cutting board roasting in the oven than overall sloth on my part.

I rationalized the situation. This couldn't be real. My mind was vacationing in Crazytown to cope with stress from work. Or my stalled love life. Or the growing stack of unpaid bills and plunging credit score. Knives can't move unless someone is holding them. If I walked into the kitchen, I'd see them all neatly stacked in the handsome wood case, the bow still attached from last Christmas.

I dove in to rescue my sanity. Maybe I startled the knives. They stopped moving when the first sock hit the linoleum. They didn't come down.

That meant I wasn't crazy. There really were knives frozen in mid-air throughout my kitchen.

I searched for the hidden camera. Any second now, a has-been celebrity would pop out of the cabinets or the fridge and reveal the hoax. We'd laugh, I'd sign a release, and it would all be over.

Nothing. It was a relief in a small way. At least I wasn't sucked into the seedy underbelly of reality TV. Dignity intact, I realized the knives were looking at me. At least I think they were looking at me. I could only assume facing down the tip of a knife was the cutlery equivalent of an intense staring contest on the schoolyard.

Logic and reason were my last resources. I approached with open, inviting body language.

"Hey. I, uh, I like your coating. Stainless steel, right?" My lips trembled from grinning so hard. I always acted so desperate when I tried to compliment someone. Something. "How about this? On the count of three, we all hit the counter, blunt end first, blade pointed away from human flesh. I'll go first. Follow my lead."

The knives didn't have a chance to cooperate. The clever made quick work of tearing into the meat of my exposed hand. My high-pitched wail sent me and the knives back in motion. Even the sink was laughing at my stupidity. Steaming water shot out of its nose into the only pot I owned.

Thank goodness my bar was in the living room. I soaked my hand in a vodka shower before wrapping it in a piece of my clean shirt. Red drops soaked the crisp linen in a Rorschach test of pain. No matter how I looked at it I saw the same thing: my body being roasted in the makeshift wood-burning stove. The wooden salad bowl and matching tongs were sacrificed in preparation for the feast.

The doorbell rang. I could only be grateful that the front door was not connected to the kitchen. An unbiased third party could mediate the conflict. Surely a pizza boy capable of that deserved a big tip and a position on the UN Security Council.

I recognized the guy from outside my window at work. He was a member of the local college's cross-country team and ran by on an almost daily basis. Perfect. If his mind failed, his body could still escape. I wondered what crime I could be charged with if the cutlery got to him before I did. There probably wasn't much legal precedent for death caused by kitchen possession.

He rang the bell again and banged on the door. I tried to be friendly. "Hey, pizza guy, right?"

He rolled his eyes. "Large pepperoni, light on the sauce for..."

"JT. Pleased to meet you. And you are...?"

"Waiting for the $13.50 so I can go to bed."

"Right. Well, listen...uh..." His name tag was blocked by my dinner.

He sighed. "It's Pete."

I smiled. "Yeah, Pete. Listen. I left my wallet in the other room. Why don't you come on in and set the pizza down." I didn't wait for an answer. He followed.

The box dropped on the floor. So much for subtlety. By the look on his face, I could tell the open floor plan betrayed his trust.

"Dude. Something's wrong with your kitchen." His eyes were wide as the ruined pepperoni.

"Tell me something I don't know, Pete." I reached out with a wrinkled twenty dollar bill as a peace offering. He didn't react. I slid the money into his apron pocket, hoping to snap him back to reality. Normalcy.

Pete shook his head twice and blinked. "I think my cousin Sheila had one of those once."

It was my turn to be shocked. "What?"

He reached down to pick up the fallen delivery and looked me straight in the eyes. "Yeah. She said it was a poltergrease or something."

"Like the movie?" Stupid question. He wasn't old enough to know the film. He wasn't even born when it first came out. "Never mind."

Pete turned back to the kitchen and stared. He scratched his head. "Hers was in the bathroom. The thing threw a toilet scrubber at her head and tried to strangle her with the shower curtain. It was messed up."

Silence. Methane permeated the air. The pot was boiling over on the stove. Spatulas flipped over the burners, melting into the sticky grease of the grates. That's when I realized Pete wanted to play hero.

Before I could warn him, he stepped into the kitchen. The kid was lucky that the butcher knife only knocked his hat off. The ladle's right hook to the eye snapped some sense into him. He screamed. He fell out of the kitchen. I think he even started to tear up.

"Dude. Why didn't you warn me?" He was in shock.

"Let me get some ice for your eye. You need it."

I reached into the bar's fridge and tossed him a chilled bottle. He pressed it to his eye. Not the way I would have used that variety of anesthetic. I wasn't going to complain if a capped bottle brought him a little relief.

I turned back to the kitchen. Pete only succeeded in making it mad. Madder. His fall knocked the pizza box to the border. It taunted both sides. The knives wouldn't go past the linoleum and I couldn't get a grip on it with the carpeting.

My sad empty stomach would have to wait. Even with the chilled bottle, Pete's eye was swelling up fast. He was struggling to keep the other one open.

"Wakey-wakey, Pete. Beauty sleep's over." He still wasn't responding. I filled a plastic cup with ice and offered it as a replacement for the bottle. He accepted. I twisted off the cap and poured out a shot. I tilted the glass into his open mouth. A spray of vodka to the face announced his return to the world of the living.

"Pete, how did your cousin get rid of the poltergeist?"

"What?" he asked. "My cousin had a what?"

"Sheila."

"Yeah, Sheila." He squinted in confusion. "How do you know her?" I slapped him right across the face. His eyes went wide and zoomed back into focus. "Dude." Success. "Not cool."

"Pete, welcome back." The pot rack crashed into the sink, pinning a trio of steak knives against the slippery surface. "How did Sheila get the thing out of her bathroom?"

"Oh that? She got my friend's grandmother to do an exorcism." He finally noticed the twenty dollar bill in his apron. "Did you need change, bro?"

"No. No change. But if you have some holy water and a priest's number handy, that'd be great." How was I supposed to do an exorcism?

"I have a bible in the back seat if that helps." Pete didn't offer an explanation. I didn't really want to know why. "I have a small crucifix in the glove compartment and rosary beads on the mirror, too, if you want them." He didn't wait for a response.

The lights began to flicker in the kitchen. Cans of soup exploded over the raging fire of the oven. A 9-1-1 call could fix that. I hoped. Better than trusting the mobile indulgence salesman out front.

Where'd I leave the phone? I checked my pockets but came up empty. I got on my knees and started looking under the bar. It had to be around here somewhere. No way was I letting that kid back in the kitchen.

There. Underneath the mini-fridge. It must have fallen when I grabbed the ice.

I dialed. One ring, two rings, three rings.

"Thank you for calling 9-1-1 emergency assistance. Unfortunately, all our lines are busy at this time. Please stay on the line and an operator will get to you as soon as possible."

"Shit." Pick up the phone. Pick it up!

The door burst open. Pete ran into the apartment carrying an armful of religious paraphernalia. He threw a Bible at me.

"Start reading, bro." What did he mean start reading?

"Pete, stop!" It was too late.

He waved his arms in front of my vodka bottle and tossed it into the kitchen. The stove erupted in flames. He ran in, screaming like a mad person.

My mouth dropped faster than the Bible from my hand. We were going to die at the hands of an invisible force and this kid was loading the shot gun and locking the hammer to the grave.

I couldn't stop him. He stepped into a knotted up rope of dishrags. With a swift tug, they flipped him upside down and dangled him from the ceiling fan. His shirt gathered around his neck. The kitchen shears made quick work of it. His half-naked torso flopped helplessly in the air.

It was no surprise when the kitchen went to work on Pete. I at least tried to be tactful when I entered. He just barged into their domain.

They certainly didn't need another chef to spoil the pot. More kitchen necessities came to life every minute. A box straight from the manufacturer spun around the room, trying to unleash the baking tools I ordered on a late night whim. The rolling pin ripped through the tape and began kneading his flesh. I was amazed the knives hadn't dulled from their nonstop assembly line of finely diced fixings from the salad bar near the office.

Each piece of equipment aimed for a feast but didn't coordinate with the rest of the line. No head chef called the shots when the kitchen ran itself.

The fan crashed to the ground. Pete grabbed his neck and crawled for the dividing line of carpeting outside the kitchen.

"Keep moving!" I reached for his hand to help pull him to safety. How cliché. He was nowhere near me yet.

A pot lid flew at my head and dropped dead once it crossed the carpeting. So did the pot dragging a tail of ripped up linoleum.

"Hurry up! They can't move outside of the kitchen!" I couldn't help but scream.

Then I actually looked at him again. The dishrags were flying about like a kite in a hurricane--wild, aiming for any calm patch in the storm. Pete dug his fingernails into the small kitchen rug and started to rise upside down. The rags caught the freezer door and improvised a tow rig.

I had no choice. I had to go back in. I grabbed the foil cutter off the bar and crossed into the war zone.

THWACK! A cast iron skillet cracked through the wall above my head. The lights started to strobe. The pan was stuck, handle caught in the light switch, desperately twitching for freedom. Great. Poltergeists and cheap haunted house clichés. A delicate balance of fact and super annoying fiction.

I got to Pete and the rug came out from under me. Literally. That stupid kitchen throw pulled me off my feet and formed a cocoon around my calves. Thank goodness for piss-poor construction. The shoddy weave was no match for my mighty foil cutter.

Pete hung above me like a prize catch at the dock save for his jackknifed neck pushing into the fridge.

"Brace yourself." The rags didn't fall as easily as the rug. I have to hand it to my family: they buy quality. I'd thank them if I got out of this alive.

The rags gave and poor Pete landed without snapping his neck. Should probably get checked out for whiplash at his soonest convenience, though. The snap-back from the fall put a sympathy crick in my neck.

The kitchen was on the offensive now. Everything not bolted down started flying right at us. Forks, flippers, and fry pans alike bravely gave their lives to the kitchen border for the chance to claim the catch of the day.

"Dude," Pete said. He had that look again like the exorcism. I think he'd hit his head a few times before winding up in my ghost story. "Make the kitchen come to us. It's, like, dying in the living room."

I lost it. "What happened the last time you provoked them? Just get out of my house before I'm answering the police about what happened to your..."

"So noble. Dude, it's cool. I'm fast."

He jumped in like a goalie and promptly got knocked out by the back end of a cleaver. The juices started to flow from his head.

I reached back in and barely saw the stock pot coming.

###

The only lingering evidence of any problem was a charred smell, like the burned out ash of charcoal at a barbecue. I couldn't believe it. The kitchen was spotless--no fire, no broken vents, no melted spatulas. Even the knives were tucked away in the wooden case, bow still attached from Christmas.

I stepped inside to get some fresh ice for my head.

Then I noticed the food: a roast, and a stew, and a plate of deep fried meat on the bone. I didn't order anything this nice.

A frying pan knocked me to the ground before a tablecloth wrapped around my throat and tied me to the lower kitchen cabinets. A paring knife and serving fork pinned my pants to the floor. I was trapped at a dinner service I didn't want an invitation to. I couldn't request a to-go order if I wanted it.

A platter dropped on my lap. My stomach turned. It was Pete's head. What remained of it, anyway.

The skull glistened—blinding white--where it had been stripped down to the ears. The remaining skin was wrinkled, like he stayed in the bath too long. The top of his skull was cracked open as a serving vessel for the lumped gray matter within.

I gagged.

Pete was dead. Fried and roasted and braised until no identifiable trace remained.

The fork dug into the cavity. I pulled my face so tight my neck twitched. The fork flew at my lips and twisted its way into my mouth.

It was warm, smooth, like scrambled eggs at a buffet.

My face relaxed after the first bite went down. The fork dropped next to my empty hand. I greedily picked it up.

He was delicious. I never had anything like him before. There was a lingering saltiness from the brine that wrecked his skin. It made my mouth water. The meat was tender and moist. I couldn't help myself.

I had seconds.

The juice dripped down my face, staining the tablecloth. I didn't care. I needed to learn the recipe--all the recipes--for everything.

The tablecloth slid to the floor without any struggle. The paring knife and fork fell over where they stood. I moved freely in my kitchen for the first time all night.

I pulled the butcher's knife from the decorative wood block. It was heavy, but easy to handle. Ergonomic, they called it. It felt right.

I was still hungry. Pizza wouldn't do. Not anymore. I checked the time. It was only 8:45. The sandwich shop would still deliver tonight.

Physics

Whatever I want in all of the world could be mine with a simple click. A twitch of a muscle will press flesh to trigger, action to history, desire to fruition.

    The offer is hard to refuse at the face of the usher. He possesses a secret hidden in the fold of his eyes. A simple crease maps out a limitless atlas of potential.

    The page descends. His hand relaxes, untwists his grip on the greatest gift of all. The glint of nail casts sparks of light against the shadowed cloak.

    And yet I do not relinquish. Could it truly be there? Could it come from this? The offer falls, picking up speed as every second passes before my eyes. The breath quickens, exhausting time on his face, in his mind, his generosity. The echo begins to fade, strike one, two, three clicks from my finger.

    Four, five, six lights descend from his hand, his fingers, glowing across my face, my neck, around his cloak. Seven, eight, nine pulses open up the eye. Ten blinks to focus on his contract. Eleven wishes for brevity. Twelve.

    The deal is done.
    He takes his fee.
    My leave is left.

Stone Cold

His fingers combed the sand. Slow at first, to adjust to the searing surface. It was only 10 AM and the sun was already brutal.

Chad knew the dry heat broke away under the loose surface. One knuckle deep and the sand was cool. This is the kind of beach Chad liked. The cooler sand didn't stick to his sunscreen. It didn't blind him with mirrored reflections of the sun. No cigarettes or broken glass, either.

Chad adjusted his sunglasses. They were too loose. They weren't his, either. He was grateful his friend Ben had an extra pair, just in case.

Chad looked at his left hand. What started as a shallow respite from the heat became a small hole, deep as his fingers. He wasn't sure when it became so big. The dull brown color betrayed the damp texture.

"Chad," Ben said. "Take of your shirt, buddy. Get some color." Ben's skin was already pocked in red. The sunscreen washed off with one swim in the ocean.

"I'm good," Chad said. "Thanks."

A pile of sand spilled onto the blanket, burying the woven binding and fringe. He kept digging.

"At least go into the water," Ben said. "We only have three days left and you only got wet in the shower." Ben dripped onto the blanket.

"I don't do ocean," Chad said. He shifted toward the sand. The little hole grew to a miniature cave. Small shells littered the walls as relics of previous inhabitants.

"Dude," Ben said. "What are you doing?"

"Digging," Chad said.

"Why?" Ben asked.

"I don't know," Chad said. "It takes my mind off of the heat."

"So would jumping in the water," Ben said.

Chad widened the hole with his right hand. Sand slid back with every movement. He could put his arm in to his elbow. The sand grew darker with every handful. The sun's gaze couldn't see around Chad's body.

He hit Ben with a fistful of sand. Ben sat up, sand caked in his hair.

"Hey!" he shouted. "Watch where you're throwing." Ben rolled off the blanket. The grains of sand slipped under his knees, knocking him face down. He spat out a mouthful of sand.

"Shh," Chad whispered. "Be quiet. I think I found something."

Ben could hardly hear his friend. He propped himself onto his elbows and walked his feet underneath him.

The hole was big. The walls were sloped, gradually getting smaller toward the bottom. Ben realized Chad hadn't whispered. His head was in the hole.

"Whoa," Ben said. He was breathless. How could the hole have grown so much so fast?

Chad pulled his head up and said, "Look. You can just catch the reflection if you look just right."

Ben leaned over the growing hole.

"Not like that!" Chad shouted. "Like this." He clawed into Ben's sunburned shoulders and repositioned his body. "Right about there. At 2:45. Hour hand."

The reflected light flipped in and out of focus as Chad waved his arm over the reflection. A tiny cap of glowing light flickered red against the graduated sand. Ben pushed the shifting grains away from the light.

A small stone broke through the surface. A gem, really. The light and beauty seemed to radiate from within. The fiery waves grew stronger in Ben's shadow.

"What is that?" Ben asked.

"What's what?" Chad pushed Ben from the hole. "I found it. I'm keeping it." Chad dove back into the hole, kicking up enough sand be covered through his chest.

The stone was longer than it looked. It radiated with all the shades of the rainbow. A cluster of colors blinded his senses as he dug deeper.

The hole grew large enough for Ben to climb in, too. Blue, green, and purple dots flew toward the flaming sky as the surface of the shore fell further away. In the distance, tiny spots of blue shifted pink and purple. A thumbnail moon was barely noticeable in the distance.

Chad and Ben didn't care. They pushed against each other, determined to stake their claim on the stone.

"There's no way you could pick it up. Just get out and leave the lifting to the real men," said Ben. He snarled at his friend, growling out threats like a cornered dog. The stone acquiesced to his touch, joining his cracked flesh. "See. It wants me."

"Like hell it does!" Chad jumped in the hole reaching the crest of yellows above Ben's head. The landing stuck. It's liked the peak of the stone was made for him. "Just let go and I'll help you out."

Ben knew he was trapped. The waves crashed closer to the hole, sprinkling the tired pair with a salty brew. He could rip out the stone and leave them both to drown or claw his way out and recover the bounty later.

But Ben's hand couldn't release. He was so close. His grip tightened against the stone, filling every gap and angle with aching flesh. He couldn't pull away if he wanted to.

Chad was in a worse spot, anyway. No matter how hard he tried, he couldn't swing off of the stone. He kicked his foot against the expanding spire and trapped leg in green. He could see the color flow into his toes.

Ben's burned shoulders marbled with the cool blues and purples overtaking his body. This proved the stone was his.

The seawater kissed the edge of the hole, breaking the heat Chad tried to escape all afternoon. The friends wrapped around the warmth of the glowing stone, twisting flesh and bone to the sand-buffed gem concealing itself in millions of grains of burning hot sand.

About the Author

I am Robert Gannon (he/him). I have run Sketching Details on various platforms for 16 years. I've worn many hats in the entertainment industry, including press, playwright, author, critic, performer, composer, designer, and educator. I'm excited to use my perspective from inside and outside of the entertainment industry to create a discussion with you about the media we consume.

Made in the USA
Middletown, DE
08 February 2025

70542132R00015